little Miss Helpful

by Roger Hargreaves

PSS!

PRICE STERN SLOAN

Little Miss Helpful was one of those people who loves to help other people, but who ends up helping nobody.

Do you know what I mean?

I mean, for instance, like the time when one of Mr. Tall's shoelaces came undone.

Now if you're as tall as Mr. Tall, tying your shoelaces isn't the easiest thing in the world.

As you can imagine!

"Let me help!" cried Little Miss Helpful, rushing up to him.

Then, somehow, she managed to tie Mr. Tall's shoelaces together.

And he fell over!

And if you're as tall as Mr. Tall, falling over hurts.

BANG!

"Ouch!" he said, rubbing his head.

"Let me help!" cried Little Miss Helpful, and rushed off to get some bandages.

And rushed back and stuck them on Mr. Tall.

Over his mouth!

"Mmmm mmmm mmm!" he said.

He was trying to say, "Take them off!"

But that's rather difficult to do with bandages stuck over your mouth.

Little Miss Helpful looked at him with concern.

"Let me help!" she cried.

And ripped the bandages off his mouth.

"Owwwwwwwwwwwwwwwwwwch!" he cried. "That hurt!"

"Would you like me to get some cream for your sore mouth?" she asked anxiously.

"No!" he groaned. "Go away!"

Now do you know what I mean about people like Little Miss Helpful who help nobody?

Last year, in April I think it was, Mr. Happy woke up feeling ill.

The doctor had to be called, and he came to Mr. Happy's house, which is on a hill, by a lake.

"Oh dear," said the doctor when he saw Mr. Happy. "Measles!"

Mr. Happy's face fell.

"Now you're to stay tucked nice and warm in bed, and get lots of rest, and take this medicine three times a day," said the doctor.

And left!

Mr. Happy settled down to sleep.

He'd just fallen asleep when there was a loud knock at his front door.

"Oh dear," groaned Mr. Happy, and staggered off to open it.

You can guess who it was.

Can't you?

"I've come to help!" she cried.

"But..." protested Mr. Happy.

"But nothing!" cried Little Miss Helpful. "Now off to bed with you, while I do some things around here!"

She looked around.

"This place needs a good cleaning," she said.

Mr. Happy had just fallen asleep again when Little Miss Helpful poked her head around his bedroom door.

"Have you got a scrub brush?" she asked.

Poor Mr. Happy had to get up and show her where it was.

And then he went back to bed.

To sleep!

Little Miss Helpful stepped back to admire the kitchen floor she'd just scrubbed.

And.

Slipped on the soap!

And.

Fell head over heels!

And.

Got her head stuck in the bucket!

And.

Because she couldn't see where she was going, walked into a shelf full of saucepans!

Which fell all over the floor, with a terrible clatter.

And.

Because she couldn't see where she was going, Little Miss Helpful stepped in one of the saucepans and got it stuck on her foot.

And.

Because she had to hop, she fell over against the refrigerator door, which flew open, and everything inside fell out!

All over Little Miss Helpful!

Poor Mr. Happy awoke with a start from the terrible commotion.

He groaned, got out of bed, went to the kitchen, and opened the door.

He couldn't believe his eyes.

There, in the middle of a pile of broken eggs, and a scrub brush, and rolling saucepans, and a lot of water, and spilt milk, and squashed butter, and bent saucepan lids, and a piece of soap, sat Little Miss Helpful!

With a bucket on her head!!

And a saucepan on her foot!!!

"Help!" came a voice from inside the bucket.

Mr. Happy grabbed the bucket, and pulled as hard as he could.

And pulled.

And pulled.

POP!

The bucket came off the top of Little Miss Helpful's head like a cork out of a bottle!

Mr. Happy shot backwards like a bullet from a gun!

Crash!

He went flying through the kitchen door!

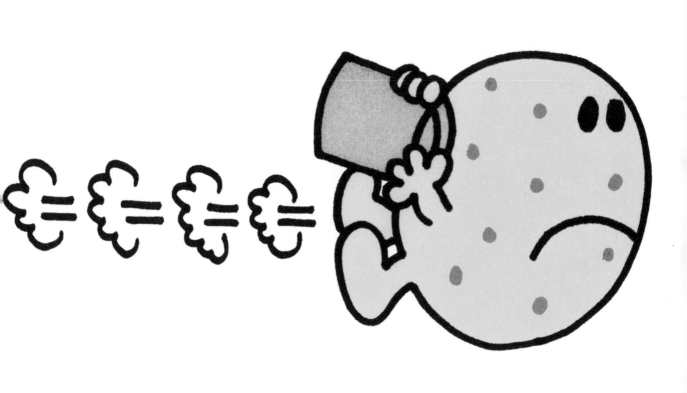

He shot across the garden, and straight through his hedge!

He rolled down the hilly field behind his garden!

Faster and faster!

And.

SPLASH!

He ended up in the lake.

With the bucket in his hand.

And a little figure, with a saucepan on one foot, came half running, half hopping, out of Mr. Happy's house.

"Let me help!" she cried.